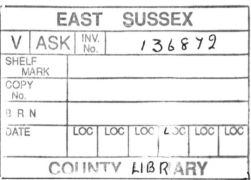

In memory of
my father

First published 1993 by
Walker Books Ltd
87 Vauxhall Walk
London SE11 5HJ

© 1993 Kim Lewis

Printed and bound in Hong Kong by
South China Printing Co. (1988) Ltd

This book has been typeset in Sabon.

British Library Cataloguing in Publication Data
A catalogue record for this
book is available from the British Library.

ISBN 0-7445-2524-1

First Snow

KIM LEWIS

WALKER BOOKS
LONDON

"Wake up, Sara," whispered Mummy. "Daddy's not very well today. I'm going to feed the sheep on the hill. Would you and Teddy like to come?"

Outside the dogs
were ready and waiting,
bright-eyed and eager to go.
Frost nipped the air. It was
early winter and the rooks
were calling. A wind was
starting to blow.

Through the gate and
up the steep track,
Mummy and Sara climbed.
The sky turned greyer and
the air grew colder.
The dogs raced on ahead.
As they climbed higher,
Sara looked back.
The farmhouse seemed
very small.

At the top of the hill
stood the lone pine tree,
bent by years of winter
winds. Mummy and Sara
stopped below it to rest.
The air went suddenly still.
"We're on top of the world,"
said Mummy, hugging
Sara. "Just you and me
and Teddy."

Across the valley the sky turned white.

Snowflakes lightly danced in the air.

"Look, look!" laughed Sara.

She watched as a snowflake fell on her mitten.

"We'd better feed the sheep," smiled Mummy,

"before it snows too hard."

Sara helped Mummy spread hay on the ground. The sheep were hungry and pushed all around them. Sara tried catching the snow in her hands, but the wind swirled the snowflakes in front of her eyes.

Then the snow fell faster
and stung Sara's cheeks.
The air grew thick and white.
"Come on," said Mummy,
her hand out to Sara.
"The sheep are all right and
we must go home before
the snow gets too deep."

The dogs disappeared through the flying snow.

Snow blotted out the lone pine.

Mummy and Sara started down the track,

hugging close to the wall.

Then suddenly Sara stopped.

"Oh no, where's Teddy?" she cried.

Mummy looked back.
Behind them the snow
was filling their tracks.
"We can't look for Teddy
now," said Mummy.
She whistled for the dogs
and started to walk, but
Sara sat still in the snow.

Then out of the whiteness,

one of the dogs appeared.

She was gently carrying Teddy.

"Oh, Teddy," cried Sara,

hugging him tight.

Mummy picked Sara and

Teddy up.

"Now we can all go home,"

she said.

As they came down the hill, the air cleared

of snow. The sky began turning blue.

Sara and Mummy could see the farmhouse

again, standing snug in the yard.

The world all around them was white and still.

Sara and Mummy
warmed up by the fire.
Then they took Daddy
his breakfast in bed.
"Who's fed the sheep?"
Daddy asked them.
Sara snuggled up
beside him.
"Mummy and Teddy
and me!" she said.